This book is given with love to...

ILLUSTRATED BY:
Vince Cleghorne
Andrew Besarab

COLORED BY:
Vince Cleghorne
Yuribelle

For my friend, Vernon...
the original Dino-Kid.

I want to be a

Dino-Kid!

I've lots of reasons why...

Like, Dino-Kids
are Dino-Huge
and almost touch
the sky.

At bedtime, Dino-Kids are never told to go to sleep...
They get to watch TV, while other kids are counting sheep.

At Dino-School,
where Dino-Kids
are taught to
scare and bite...
They get to go in
when they please,
the afternoon
or night.

When bath time comes around,
a Dino-Kid rejects the tub...
They find themselves a swimming pool,
to have a soapy scrub.

When asked to eat his greens,
a Dino-Kid will frown and then...
Eat the trees at a public park,
so he's never asked again.

When Dino-Kids get really sick,
the doctors always say...
"It's best to eat a Dino-Burger,
to keep the germs away."

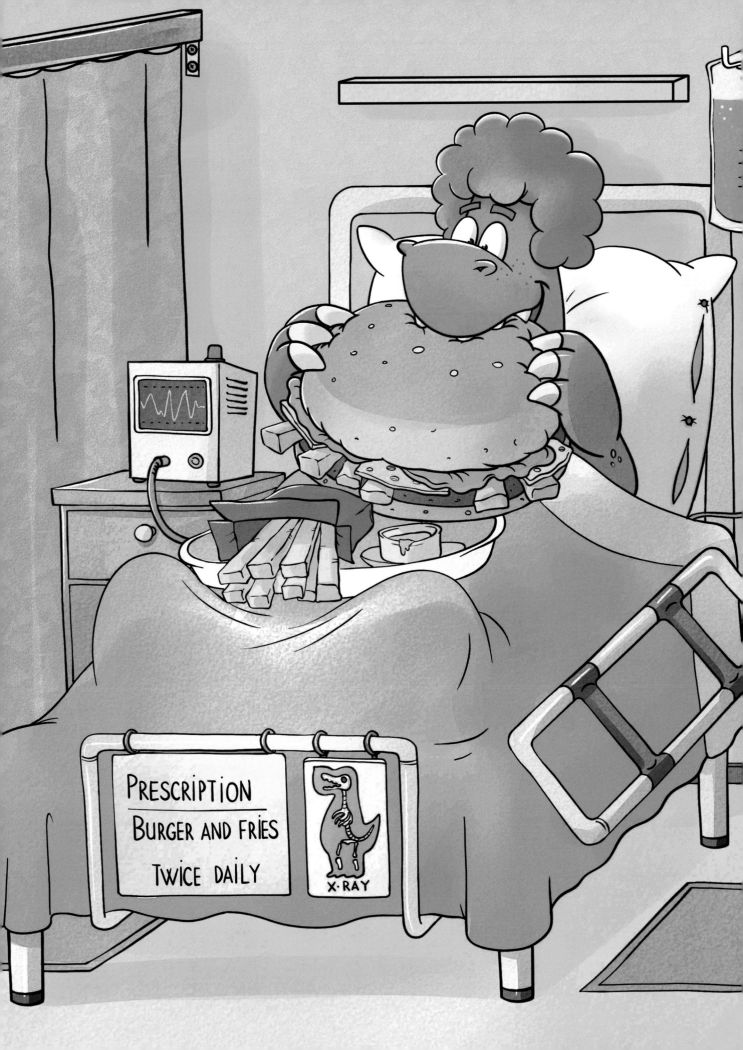

And when his shots are due,
a Dino-Kid will grin...
"No needle is strong enough,
to pierce my scaly skin!"

When hordes of spooky ghosts decide,
to creep around at night...
A Dino-Kid will roar so loud,
they disappear with fright.

When visiting the barber,
Dino-Kids put on a show...
By hiring helicopters,
for their monthly trim and blow.

On Halloween, a Dino-Kid,
will always be the one..
To win "Best Monster Costume",
though he doesn't have one on.

If he's told "Go clean your room!",
a Dino-Kid will say...
"No problem," as he lifts the house,
and tips the mess away.

And even shorter Dino-Kids, are guaranteed a ride...
As they're a whole lot taller, than the height restriction guide.

When playground bullies think to themselves,
they've scored an easy lunch...
A Dino-Kid will knock them flat,
without a single punch.

I want to be a Dino-Kid,
so please don't make a peep...
'Cause I can be a Dino-Kid
when I am fast asleep!

THE END

Dino-Kid Activity Sheets

We hope you liked reading the story of I want to be A Dino-Kid.
Please enjoy the bonus drawing pages we've included
for you to create your own Dino-Kid and color in the original!
Don't forget to include your name and age below
to help remember when you drew this.

Name: _____

Age: _____   Date: _____

Draw Yourself as a Dino-Kid

What would you do? How big would you be?

🐾 Claim Your FREE Gift!

Visit ➡ PDICBooks.com/dinokid

Thank you for purchasing I want to be a Dino-Kid, and welcome to the Puppy Dogs & Ice Cream family.

We're certain you're going to love the little gift we've prepared for you at the website above.